Babies in Toyland

KLASKY CSUPO INC.

Based on the TV series *Rugrats*® created by Arlene Klasky, Gabor Csupo,
and Paul Germain as seen on Nickelodeon®

SIMON SPOTLIGHT

An imprint of Simon & Schuster Children's Publishing Division
1230 Avenue of the Americas, New York, New York 10020
Copyright © 2002 Viacom International Inc. All rights reserved.
NICKELODEON, *Rugrats,* and all related titles, logos,
and characters are trademarks of Viacom International Inc.

Printed in Mexico

First Edition
2 4 6 8 10 9 7 5 3 1

ISBN 0-689-85228-2

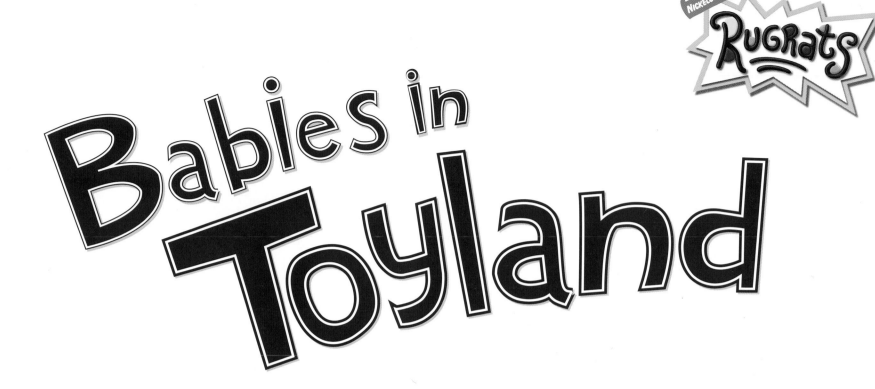

Babies in Toyland

adapted by Sarah Willson
based on the teleplay by Eryk Casemiro
illustrated by Robert Roper and Bob Ostrom

Simon Spotlight/Nickelodeon

New York   London   Toronto   Sydney   Singapore

It was the grand opening of Christmasland, and Stu Pickles was giving his family and friends a tour.

"I don't like to brag," Stu said modestly, "but the work I've done here will put Pickles Industries on the map!"

Angelica pushed past the babies. "Outta my way, tinselheads!" she said. "I'm going to see Santa right now!"

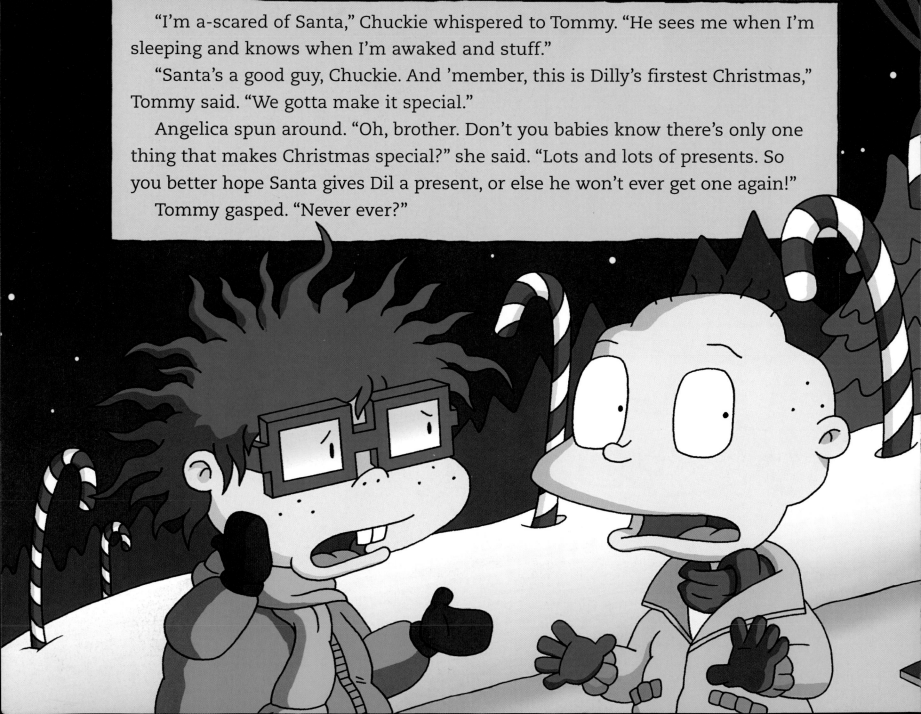

"I'm a-scared of Santa," Chuckie whispered to Tommy. "He sees me when I'm sleeping and knows when I'm awaked and stuff."

"Santa's a good guy, Chuckie. And 'member, this is Dilly's firstest Christmas," Tommy said. "We gotta make it special."

Angelica spun around. "Oh, brother. Don't you babies know there's only one thing that makes Christmas special?" she said. "Lots and lots of presents. So you better hope Santa gives Dil a present, or else he won't ever get one again!"

Tommy gasped. "Never ever?"

"I can hardly wait to see this 'brilliant' design work of yours, bro," said Drew with a snort.

Stu motioned to a computer screen. "One flip of a switch, and you have the Nutcracker battling the Mouse King! Over here is the little town of Bethlehem with a petting zoo! And with this knob here I can make real snow! It goes from FLURRY to BLIZZARD with a touch of a button," he said. "Come on, let's take a ride on the Christmasland Express!"

"You folks go on ahead," said Grandpa Lou. "I'll stay here with the sprouts."

TOWN OF BETHLEHEM PIONEER CABIN NUTCRACKER GROVE

NATIVITY PETTING ZOO SANTA'S WORKSHOP SNOW MAKER

As the grown-ups boarded the train, no one noticed a spark fly out of the snow machine. Then another spark flew out. The needle crept toward BLIZZARD.

"I'm going to find Santa," Angelica announced as she stomped off.

"We'd better follow her and find Santa afore he runs out of prezzies," said Lil.

"Yeah, and before Grandpa Lou wakes up from his nap," added Phil.

"Santa Claus!" yelled Angelica when she spotted a man in a red suit. "I've been looking all over for you!"

"Uh, ho-ho-ho, little girl," he said. "I don't start my shift for five more minutes."

"Well, we may as well get started," said Angelica. "I want a Commercial Pilot Cynthia set, and a purple bicycle with flowered training wheels, and—"

"Whoa, hold on!" Santa interrupted. "Uh, let's see what Santa has for you. Close your eyes."

Angelica felt Santa place something in her hands, and she opened her eyes. "That's *it?!*" She yelled. "A stupid *moose?*"

"It's a *reindeer*," Santa said. "And it's the thought that counts."

"Well, I'm thinking this present stinks!" Angelica cried.

"Oh, yeah?" Santa snapped back. "Well, you can kiss Christmas good-bye, because I . . . I *quit!*" He threw down his hat and stalked off.

"Tommy?" said Chuckie. "If Santa quitted, does that mean we're not getting presents?"

Tommy nodded gravely. "And even worse, it means that Dil isn't going to gets to have another Christmas ever again!"

"But when Santy quitted, he didn't have his big bag of presents with him," Kimi said. "Maybe it's still at the North Pole!"

Hmm . . . she's right! Angelica thought. Where there's a North Pole, there's elfs makin' toys. Lots of 'em—all for me! But first I gotta get these babies out of the way.

"Hey!" she called to the babies. "The North Pole is that way!" And she pointed in the wrong direction.

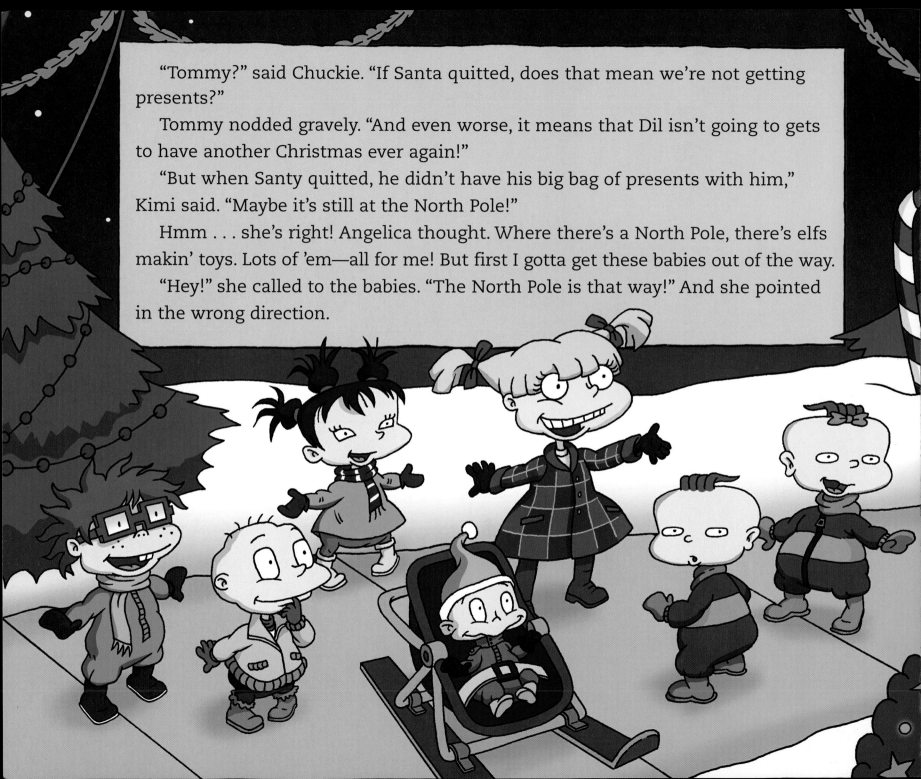

Meanwhile, the grown-ups had arrived at the first train stop.

"Welcome to Little Christmas on the Prairie!" Stu said proudly.

The grown-ups wandered around the pioneer cabin. "Everything in here looks the way it did when I was a girl!" said Lulu. "It's even snowing outside!"

Snow was piling up quickly on the windowsill.

Drew rattled the door handle. "It's stuck!" he cried. "Thanks to your silly snow machine, we're snowed in!"

The babies were lost near a grove of fake trees. "What's this?" asked Chuckie, looking down at a huge, fake walnut. As he stooped to pick it up he accidentally brushed against a switch. "Aaaaah!" yelled the babies as a giant nutcracker began marching their way.

A ballerina began to twirl. Her shoe flew off, and Phil caught it. Lil found herself holding a piece of satin ribbon.

Then Chuckie got tangled up with the Mouse King's toy sword just as an army of mice scampered out of the woods. One of their hats flew off and landed on Dil's head. Kimi caught a jingle bell.

Chuckie's snowsuit ripped, and he fell into a pile of snow.

"Let's get outta here!" called Tommy. They jumped onto Dil's stroller and swooshed down the snowy hill toward Bethlehem.

Back at the cabin, the grown-ups were making the best of their snowed-in Christmas Eve.

"I have to admit," said Charlotte, "there is a certain antiquated charm to this nonsense. More popcorn, guys!" she shouted to Drew and Chas, who were popping corn over the open hearth.

Stu handed Lulu the ornament he had made.

"It's perfect, Stuart!" cried Lulu. "This angel will go on the top of our tree!"

"This doesn't look like the North Pole," said Tommy as he and the other babies rolled to a stop at the bottom of a hill.

"Look, you guys!" Lil cried. "A baby!"

"It must be *your* first Christmas too," Kimi said to the baby. "Too bad Santa quitted, and you don't get any presents."

"You can have my ribbie!" said Lil, placing her ribbon next to the baby.

"And my shoe!" said Phil.

"And my jingly," said Kimi.

"All right, you can have my Christmas walbnut," sighed Chuckie.

Even Dil offered the baby a present. As Tommy placed Dil's hat on its head the mechanical baby moved.

"Hey, guys, he's smilin' at us!" said Tommy.

NATIVITY PETTING ZOO

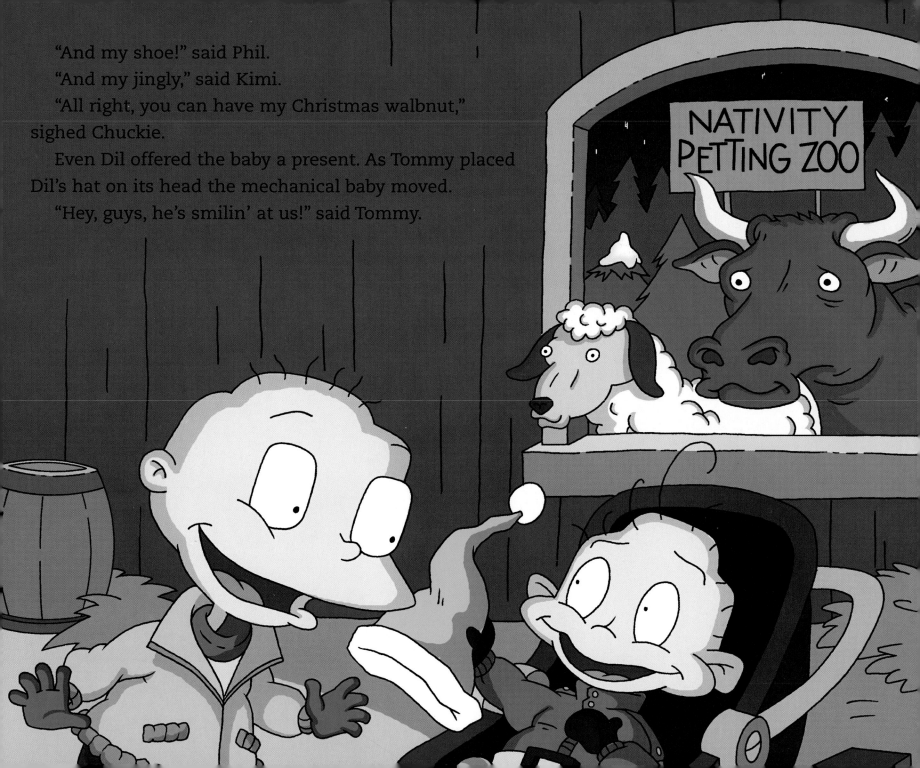

On the other side of Christmasland, Angelica had finally reached the North Pole. She pulled her toy reindeer out of her pocket. "Do you think we're near Santa's workshop, Prancy?" she asked it.

She peered through a window. Inside, little robot elves were busy making toys. She banged on the door, and then suddenly . . .

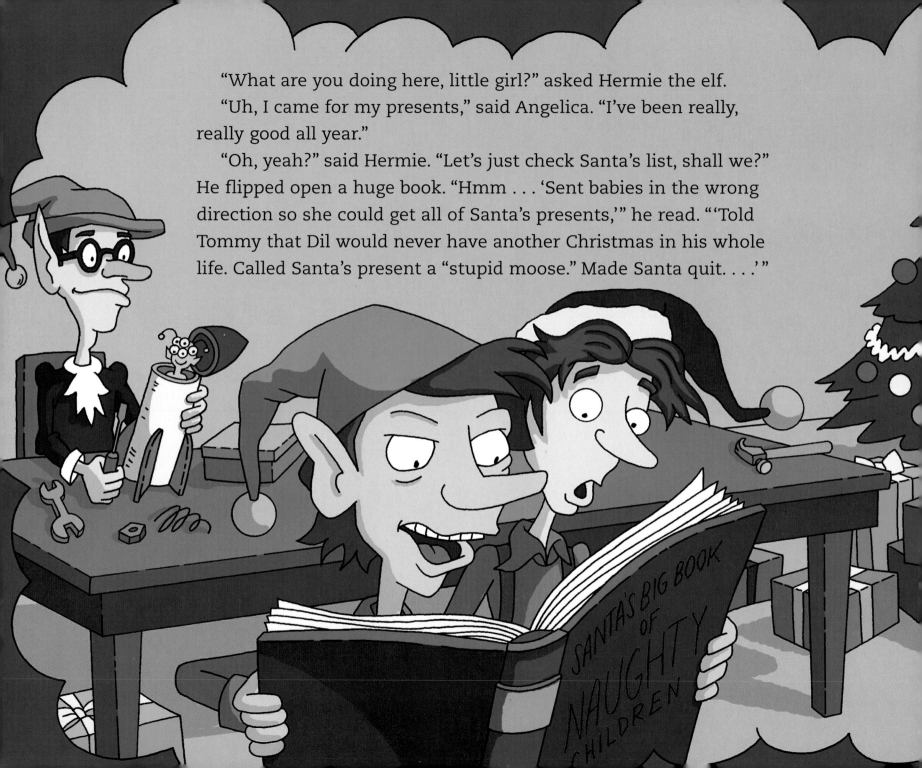

"What are you doing here, little girl?" asked Hermie the elf.

"Uh, I came for my presents," said Angelica. "I've been really, really good all year."

"Oh, yeah?" said Hermie. "Let's just check Santa's list, shall we?" He flipped open a huge book. "Hmm . . . 'Sent babies in the wrong direction so she could get all of Santa's presents,'" he read. "'Told Tommy that Dil would never have another Christmas in his whole life. Called Santa's present a "stupid moose." Made Santa quit. . . .'"

SANTA'S BIG BOOK
of
NAUGHTY
CHILDREN

Angelica heard a scratching sound and turned. "Prancy!" she cried.
"You're real!"

Prancy backed away. "You called me stupid?!" cried Prancy. "I thought
we were friends."

"Oh, Prancy! I didn't mean it!" said Angelica. "I'm sorry!"

She blinked back a tear, and the toy reindeer appeared again in her
hand. "From now on I'll be good, Prancy," she whispered to it. "At least,
I'll try."

Back at Bethlehem, the babies heard a jingling of bells. "There you sprouts are!" called Grandpa Lou from a sleigh. "I heard an elf say some babies were on the loose. Must have snuck off while I rested my eyes! Hmm . . . we're a half-pint short. Let's find Angelica and then track down those folks of yours!"

As Grandpa Lou loaded them into the sleigh, the babies glanced back at the baby in the manger one last time.

From inside the cabin, Christmas carols could be heard.

"I'd know that piano-playing anywhere!" said Lou. He hopped out of the sleigh and began shoveling.

"Merry Christmas, babies!" came a voice from behind. Angelica walked toward them with her arms full of gifts.

"You finded Santa's workshop?" asked Lil.

"Yeah, and I'm so good, I'm practically an elf now!" Angelica said as she handed out presents to the babies.

The babies exchanged surprised glances.

Angelica realized she was one present short. She held Prancy close. "I'm gonna miss you," she said as she handed Dil the reindeer. "Here you go, drooly," she said. "Take good care of him."

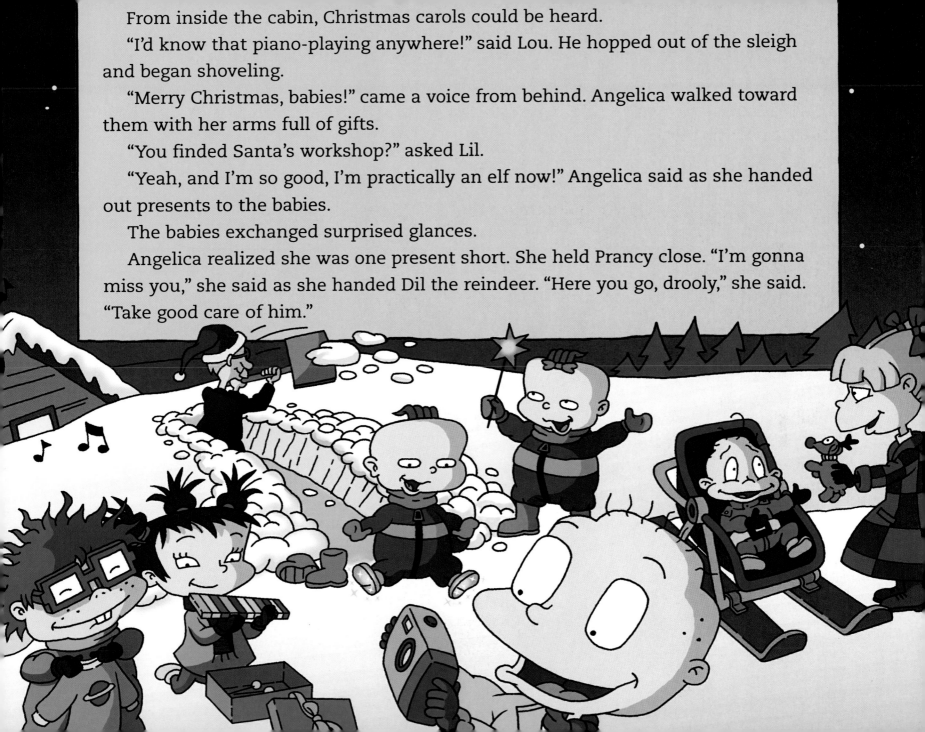

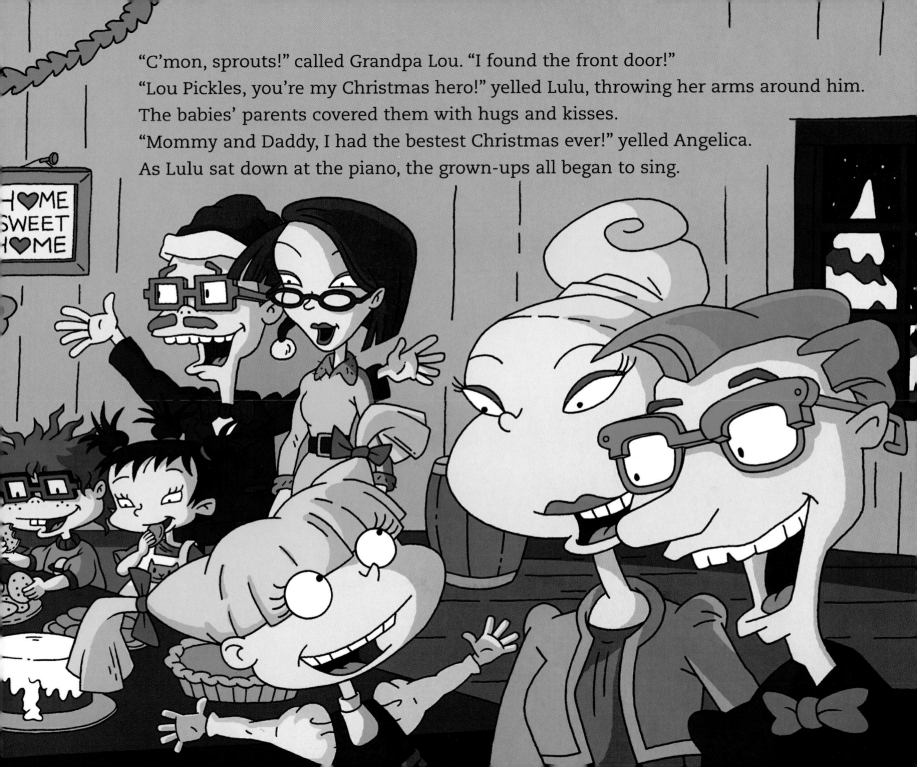

"C'mon, sprouts!" called Grandpa Lou. "I found the front door!"
"Lou Pickles, you're my Christmas hero!" yelled Lulu, throwing her arms around him.
The babies' parents covered them with hugs and kisses.
"Mommy and Daddy, I had the bestest Christmas ever!" yelled Angelica.
As Lulu sat down at the piano, the grown-ups all began to sing.

HOME
SWEET
HOME

"Tommy," whispered Chuckie. "Don'cha think we had a good time tonight? Even before we gots any presents?"

"Yeah," agreed Tommy. "Maybe doing stuff together is what makes Christmas special, huh?"

"Let's take a Christmas picture with your new picture taker!" said Kimi.

Tommy held the camera out in front of the babies. "Okay, everybody . . . say 'PEAS!'"